THE BEAST OF MONSIEUR RACINE

Tomi Ungerer

M

MACMILLAN CHILDREN'S BOOKS

DEDICATION : *to Maurice Sendak*

First published in 1972 by The Bodley Head Limited

Picturemac edition published 1987 by
Macmillan Children's Books
A division of Macmillan Publishers Limited
London and Basingstoke
Associated companies throughout the world

British Library Cataloguing in Publication Data
Ungerer, Tomi
    The beast of Monsieur Racine.——(Picturemac)
    I. Title
    823'.914[J]   PZ7
    ISBN 0-333-43926-0

Printed in Hong Kong

Monsieur Racine was a retired tax collector who lived peacefully in a secluded cottage. He was content to spend his days shuffling about, watching birds and clouds, and tinkering with his little garden.

In this garden grew a pear tree which was Monsieur Racine's great pride. It bore fruit of extraordinary flavour and juiciness.

Pears from that tree had won him many prizes at local country fairs. Millionaires had offered great sums of money for his harvest.

"What do I want with all that money?" he thought. "The pears are mine, I love them, I eat them." There was no selling, there was no sharing. Monsieur Racine was a happy man.

But one morning, alas! three times, alas! he found all his pears gone.

Upon closer investigation, he discovered strange footprints the predator had left behind. Footprints of a weird nature, indeed. It looked as if the ground had been trampled by stumps rather than feet.

"Outrageous, positively outrageous!" exclaimed the victim. "Only a young elephant could have left such tracks."

One pear was still dangling from a high branch. "Ah-ha! One pear left!" said Monsieur Racine. "I am sure the marauder will come back for it. And I shall be here to give out the proper punishment."

He fetched some yarn and tied one end to the golden pear, the other to the bell hanging in the cottage entrance. Then he put on his old cavalry uniform and squeezed himself into its shiny cuirass. Facing the open door, he waited all day, his sabre at the ready.

Hours dropped by and Monsieur Racine fell asleep.

It was dusk when suddenly the bell started to jingle nervously. Our avenger jumped to his feet and grabbed his sabre. "*Sapristi!*"

There in the twilight stood a beast, the strangest thing Monsieur Racine had ever set eyes upon.

It was large, about the size of a young calf.

From a distance it looked like a heap of mouldy blankets. Long, sock-like ears were flopping on both sides of a seemingly eyeless head. A shaggy, mangled mane topped a drooping snout. Its feet were like stumps, and it had baggy knees. It made no sound.

Monsieur Racine's anger gave way to curiosity. "It looks inoffensive enough," he muttered to himself as he came out of the cottage. The beast didn't budge and even seemed willing to strike up an acquaintance. So Monsieur Racine pulled a macaroon out of his pocket and, mounting it on the tip of his blade, presented it to the thing.

The friendly offering was acknowledged.

"More delicacies of this sort and it could be tamed," reflected Monsieur Racine. He went to his kitchen and fetched a wedge of apple tart, salami, pâté, and a bottle of red wine.

Man and beast picnicked heartily under the pear tree.

It was late and dark when the animal got up to depart. "Good night, gentle thing," said Monsieur Racine as he kissed his visitor on both jowls. "Come back tomorrow and we shall have a lovely time together."

Late every afternoon the beast came back, and every night it vanished into the forest it had come from.

It was especially fond of cookies, chocolate, and ice-cream. So eager was Monsieur Racine to please his guest that he installed, at great expense, a refrigeration system, to preserve vats of ice-cream delivered from the city.

On rainy days, they would just be cosy on the old sofa Monsieur Racine had inherited from his Aunt Sophie. Both friends enjoyed music. They listened religiously.

''I lost my pears but found a companion,'' thought the old tax collector.

On sunny days, when road conditions would allow it, he would load the beast in a trailer pulled by his motricycle. Off they zoomed with dizzying speed.

The animal was playful and Monsieur Racine built a whole playground for its rompings.

Some sight it was when the old man and his pet frolicked all over the place.

All the while, Monsieur Racine was studying the
creature, taking photographs, making sketches, recording
measurements. He found it unrelated to any other living
form. Bodily tissues were lifeless, the bone structure was
nonexistent. The whole body seemed to consist of a
conglomerate of living lumps.

Monsieur Racine searched his library for a hint. Nothing.
This beast was unheard of.

So Monsieur Racine decided to write to the Academy of
Sciences in Paris. With his letter he enclosed a meticulous
study of the animal's living habits, as well as a set of
photographs.

The answer was prompt. Monsieur Racine's discovery
had created a sensation among the members of the Academy,
and he was invited to Paris to present his find.

He went to work at once. With the help of his creature,
he built a comfortable cage.

It was carted at government expense to the nearest railway station.

Their arrival in Paris was a triumph. The Mayor himself
insisted on welcoming the new French wonder.

Military bands escorted our friends to their hotel.
Reporters and photographers were everywhere.

Fortunes were offered for Monsieur Racine's animal by circus owners, zoo managers, and wealthy maniacs. "What do I want with money?" was his answer. "The beast is my friend, and friends are not for sale. And let that be that!"

The next day was *the* day.

The members of the Academy met in the amphitheatre. At ten o'clock Greenwich time, the door to the platform opened and Monsieur Racine walked in, fittingly dressed in a dark suit and followed by the beast.

There were Ohs and Ahs from the audience and unanimous applause. Some ladies swooned.

On the platform Monsieur Racine was now ready to make his presentation. "Messieurs, mesdames, honoured members of the Academy . . ."

THEN something incredible happened.

The beast, which had always remained silent, broke into hysterical giggles. Shaking, rolling on its side, it ripped and tore itself apart.

Out of a pile of skins and rags emerged two children. The assembly was struck dumb and numb, then burst into an uproar. The police had to be called in to clear the amphitheatre.

When news of the hoax reached the crowds waiting
outside, a riot began. Buses were overturned.

Unspeakable acts were performed.
What a mess! People are still talking about it.

But Monsieur Racine, who had a sense of humour, found the joke quite unique. After congratulating the children for their cleverness and endurance, he took them on a tour of the capital.

Then they went home and the children were returned to their parents, nice country folk who lived on the other side of the forest.

Monsieur Racine soon had a new crop of pears, which he happily shared with his two young friends.